Irene Ackerman

Inez

A drama in three acts

Irene Ackerman

Inez
A drama in three acts

ISBN/EAN: 9783337343828

Printed in Europe, USA, Canada, Australia, Japan

Cover: Foto ©Andreas Hilbeck / pixelio.de

More available books at **www.hansebooks.com**

INEZ.

A DRAMA IN THREE ACTS.

BY IRENE ACKERMAN.

NEW YORK:

CHARLES H. BAUER, PUBLISHER,

148TH STREET, NEAR THIRD AVENUE.

INEZ.

DRAMATIS PERSONÆ.

I N E Z.

COUNT DIEGO.

BARON ENGALTARE.

JUAN DE PLATA.

DENNIS.

LAWYER CUMMINGS.

EXPRESSMAN.

LANDLORD.

FATHER CREGAN.

CAPTAIN OF THE GUARD.   OFFICER OF THE DAY.

SOLDIERS.   NOTARY.   CLERKS.   MESSENGER.

THE AMERICAN MINISTER.   CLERGYMAN.

RUFFIANS.   CONVICTS.   ROBBERS, AND HOTEL SERVANTS.

Events occur in New York, London, and Spain.   Period 1879.

Costumes modern.

Act I. Scene I. *The home of* INEZ, *a room in a tenement house in New York.*

New Saratoga trunk at C.

Inez, *discovered sleeping, seated in a chair, with her arm under her head at a table R.*

———

(Soft Music.)

INEZ [waking] Was it a dream ?
It seems even now to be real.
I dreamt.
This is no time for dreaming.

I am here yet. In this room for the last time. Now, and here, to end a life of want and suffering. To be no longer the child of poverty's hovel. (*Going towards the trunk.*) But Inez the great Soprano. *Opens the trunk.*) And by your aid to enter a world, I dreamed, prayed, and longed to reach. No longer to live in a hole like this. In rags like these. (*Looking at her dress.*)

But (*speaking to the trunk*) out from you to get these satins, velvets, silks and laces. These soft kid gloves from France, and boots from Spain, to decorate myself, and move where proud men shall bend to kiss my hand, and prouder women courtesy as I enter.

By your aid, and my voice I'll upward soar ; the past forgetting in the triumphs of the future.

Oh! my magic treasure! (*Embraces the trunk,*) How I love you!

Not as silly maid loves dress. Oh! no. But as new made knight his armor loves, so love I you. You are my armor. The stage my field. Poverty my foe. You and I will win the fight.

I have worked and toiled to get you. I have sung in places I abhorred to gather coins for you. I have kept my very body cold and hungry often here to own you. Without you I was weak. With you I am strong. Now you'are mine. Mine with all'your treasures.

Come, exert your magic power. Change me. Make all that know me, never know me more. And all that see me pay me homage.

Change me from this (*looking at her dress*).

And when changed, I'll stand, I'll walk. Aye!!! and rule a queen.

(*Commences to undress.*)

(*Shut in quick.*)

ACT I. SCENE II. *Street in New York City.*

Enter DENNIS.

DENNIS—It's a hard thing to be out of work. Hard on the man, but harder on the wife, and children (when you have them. It's a comfort, anyways, I have none of them). The legs are wore off of me looking for a place. (*Takes the Herald out of his pocket—Reads.*)

"Wanted by a respectable man who can bring the best city re "ferences,—Situation as coachman, footman, or butler. Eight years "in last place. Now out of employment; family having gone to Eu- "rope. Address Dinnis, Herald office."

I put that in the paper. Five cents a word, and every word the truth.

Enter EXPRESSMAN.

EXPRESMAN— Mimicing him. "Address DINNIS."

Why didn't you say address James, or Thomas? Something English, or French, but DINNIS? I thought you had more sense. That's too Irish. We want style at the door.

*DENNIS,—*True for you. Style is more in demand now than ould-fashioned honesty.

EXPRESSMAN,—"Ould-fashioned honesty?" You'll want knee-breeches, and no greenbacks—and nothing but gold and good manners next. Arrah! why don't you set up for a dry nurse, and teach children? I'm surprised at you. No wonder you don't get a place.

*DENNIS,—*No wonder when the likes of you does.

*EXPRESSMAN,—*Dennis, where are you living?

*DENNIS,—*Where I always lived—

*EXPRESSMAN,—*Oh! get out—what year is it?

*DENNIS,—*Eighteen hundred and seventy-nine, —of course since the first of January.

*EXPRESSMAN,—*Oh! I see you know that. But you don't know that the electric light has outed the candles your mother had, and that—

*DENNIS,—*I'll knock the daylights out of you, if you give me any more of your lip. Who gave you the right to talk thus to your betters?

*EXPRESSMAN,—*Don't get mad, Dennis! I like you.

*DENNIS,—*You like me? What next I'd like to know; may be you'll be asking for a favor next, after making a morning's sport of me—

*EXPRESSMAN,—*Come, let's make up. Do you know of any one that wants any hauling done?

*DENNIS,—*Keep a civil tongue in your head, young man, for the future—you don't know when it may serve you. Here you are abusing a man that can give you a job as little as you thought it.

*EXPRESSMAN,—*If you'll find the job I'll find the beer.

*DENNIS,—*When I wants beer I buys it; but if you want any hauling, the girl that lives in the room next to me wants a trunk taken to the depot at twelve, and it's near that now.

*EXPRESSMAN,—*I'll be there for it.

*DENNIS,—*She wanted a hack too.

*EXPRESSMAN,—*I'll bring a hack when I come.

DENNIS,—Now you got a job; tell me where I can get one.

EXPRESSMAN,—(*pretends to be in deep thought.*) I don't see exactly,—Coney Island is closed, or you might apply for footman to the midgets.

DENNIS,—To whom?

EXPRESSMAN,—Never mind to who? That situation won't be open till summer.—It's a pity you are an Irishman.

DENNIS,—"Pity I'm an Irishman?" and is it the likes of you that tills me that?

EXPRESSMAN,—Oh! get out! Don't you see that Irishmen are only used to put others in office? Now if you were a native, I might get some of my friends to make you an Alderman, or—

DENNIS,—A native? I'm as good a man as any native in the Bowery, or out of it.

EXPRESSMAN,—Yes, Oh! yes; you look like it—we ought to have more of your pictures.—Why don't you get married and give us a few?

DENNIS,—Me take a wife? why I can't support myself now, much less a wife.

EXPRESSMAN,—Support a wife! That's another of your old-fashioned notions. Support a wife—what for? Make her go to work, and support you? That's the way some of us, natives, and some of the intelligent foreigners do.

DENNIS,—Support me—why should she?

EXPRESSMAN,—Because she's a woman, and you ought to take your ease, except when you like to work. Because it's her business to to do whatever you like. Because you can make her, for you're the strongest.

DENNIS,—Ain't you afraid that "dacent baste" of a horse you drive would kick the head off of you, and such sentiments as them out of you? I think he would if he knowed it. Now look here, my chap. I have stood your chaff long enough; but if you open your mouth again a woman in my presence I'll make a native corpse of you. Bad luck to me, but I will—

EXPRESSMAN,—Get out, you foreigner!

DENNIS,—A foreigner! Me a foreigner? *Throwing off his coat to fight the* EXPRESSMAN, I'll show you who you call a foreigner—

EXPRESSMAN,—See if you can catch up with the wagon. You foreign bondholder!

Exits.

DENNIS,—(*Putting on his coat*) A foreign what? What's that he called me? If ever I get my eye on him, and the police ain't nigh, I'll punch that head of his till I learn him to know an Irishman, and a democrat at that from a foreigner.

Exits.

Scene shifted.

Act I. Scene III.— *The same room in the garret; INEZ standing near the trunk, magnificently dressed, walking costume.*

(*Raps at door.*)

INEZ,—Come in.

Enter LANDLORD.

LANDLORD,—I was looking for the girl that lives here.

INEZ,—Are you the landlord?

LANDLORD,—Yes, lady; her month is up to-day. I called for the rent.

INEZ,—Here is money she left with me for you. (*Hands him money*) See if it is right. She has left for good. I got her a better position. I only waited for you to come, and the man to take this trunk,—she has been making some clothes for me. I forgot I will have to stay until the man comes who is to get these things (*points to the furniture*). Is the money right?

LANDLORD,—All right, ma'm. When you go out leave the key in the door. I'll be back in an hour (*As he is going.*)

INEZ,—If you see the expressman send him up. Please tell the hackman I will be down soon.

LANDLORD, (*Obsequiously*)—Delighted to serve you, ma'm; I'm glad the girl has got a better place ; she was a good tenant, paid her rent punctual,—a good girl,—though a little airy sometimes,—proud-like, but a very good girl. Put the key in the door as you go out, ma'm. (*Going, turns.*) May be you'd like me to stop to help you, ma'm?

INEZ,—No, thank you.

LANDLORD,—Good day, ma'm. Leave the key in the door. Good day, ma'm! *Exits.*

INEZ (*Laughing*),—Well, that's done. That's done. He never knew me. Spoke better of me than I expected. (*Tapping the trunk,*) You have changed me.

(*Raps.*)
Come in—
Enter EXPRESSMAN.

EXPRESSMAN,—We were told to come here for a trunk.

INEZ,—There it is, take it to the Grand Central depot. Wait there until I come. *They are carrying the trunk out.* DENNIS *Enters.*

EXPRESSMAN *and* DENNIS *make faces at each other, as they pass.*

DENNIS to INEZ,—Beg pardon, Miss. Where's the girl gone that lives here? There's a hack below waiting for her—

INEZ,—She wanted it for me; she has gone earlier than she expected. I got her an excellent position. Are you the man called Dennis, that lives in the next room?

DENNIS,—Yes, Miss.

INEZ,—She told me to give you all these things, and this money as a keepsake, and to say good-bye for her.

DENNIS,—God bless her wherever she goes. An honest good girl she always was, and Oh! the illegant voice she has!

INEZ,—Tell me all about her.

DENNIS,—Well, you see, Miss, I hear she was an orphan child when she was five years old—an ould Italian fiddler that was a great musician took charge of her; and raised her [what raising she got in this house). He taught her music, and singing. Between him and the public schools she got her education. He polished the beautiful voice God gave her, but he almost broke the child's heart with his outlandish ways, he was so cross. One thing I'll say for him. He sent her to the dancing school. There's where she got that style and grand walk of hers. And he brought her up a good Catholic, Miss.

INEZ,—Where is he now?

DENNIS,—Dead. God rest his soul! Well, Miss, she then went out by herself to earn her living.

INEZ,—How?

DENNIS,—She took to singing. Sometimes in the saloons and gardens, then in the Varieties, until one day when my poor old mother was dying in the next room. While the priest was giving me mother the last rites she sat here singing. The sound of her voice went in and round the dying woman, like an angel's singing, and made her smile even as she died. When we had closed my mother's eyes [*weeps*] Father Creegan asked me who was that singing. So I ups and tells him. "Dennis," says he, "if we could only get her to sing in the chapel, 't would be the making of us," says he. 'Why don't you ask her?' says I. "An' I will," says the priest.

INEZ,—What then?

DENNIS,—In here we comes, and the priest asks her fair and easy like.

INEZ,—What did she say?

DENNIS, (Laughing)—Father, says she, I'll sing for a trial for nothing, but if I suit I'll want pay for my singing, as well as you do for the services.

INEZ,—Oh! didn't the priest get vexed at that?

DENNIS,—Not he. He laughed hearti y. "That's fair,' says he. Come and sing for the Virgin and me," says he, "and if you sing in the chapel like you sang that Ave Maria just now, you will fill the chapel with rich people, and I'll raise the pew rent on them. Then I'll give you ten cents on every dollar of the raise," says he. 'It's a bargain, Father,' says she. So next Sunday she sang, Miss; and such singing was never heard at Mass before. The priest raised the pew rents instanter. He got the money, that's more. Then after awhile he raised them higher, and higher. The chapel was crowded, and the plates piled up with the money in them. She and the pew rent kept rising higher and higher. And now, glory be to us all! Father Cregan is a made man, and building a new church, and the Cardinal asks him to dinner. Allowing to the blessing of heaven, and that illigant, sweet voice of hers. That's the truth; and now when she was doing so well, she's gone! We'll all miss the darling good girl, but the chapel will miss her most. She was too good for the likes of us.

INEZ, (As if a sudden thought strikes her) Aside,—Why cannot I take Dennis with me? He could be my servant. In his new mistress he never will recognize the Inez he knew. I would feel safer. I must arrange it. He shall go.

DENNIS,—Do all you can for her, Miss.

INEZ,—I will indeed. Good-bye! [*Goes to the door; turns.*] Good bye! I will tell her how kindly you spoke of her. Perhaps I may engage you myself. Good bye for her!

[*Picture*] *INEZ* at the door.

DENNIS [*falling on his knees*],—Oh! Blessed Virgin! Shield her wherever she goes.

CURTAIN.

*Act II. Scene I. *Hotel in England.*

BARON ENGALTARE S Room. *BARON an invalid disco-vered sitting in a large arm chair. LAWYER CUMMINGS at the table opposite the Baron, with a lawyer's green bag, by him—on the table pens, and ink, a little bell, &c., &c.*

Baron,—Have you prepared the deeds and my will, as I directed?

Lawyer, [*Takes papers from bag,*]—Yes, here they are. There is a blank line in each. When that is filled with the name of the person you wish, and you execute them the matter is finished I have a notary and two clerks as witnesses in waiting.

Baron,—Put the will aside for the present. Now fill the blanks you spoke of with the name of Inez De Plata of New York, daughter of my beloved friend, Juan De Plata.

Lawyer, (*Looks astonished.*)

Baron,—Cannot I do this?

Lawyer,—Most assuredly. (*Writes in each deed.*)

Baron,—When I have executed and delivered these papers to Mademoiselle, does not all the property enumerated in each of the deeds immediately become hers?

Lawyer,—The moment she takes the deeds from you the property is no longer yours, it then becomes hers.

Baron,—That is what I desire. Now I am ready; call the witnesses.

Lawyer, (*rings*).

Enter Servant.

To Servant,—Tell the gentlemen waiting to come up.

Exit Servant.

Enter NOTARY and CLERKS.

Baron,—Gentlemen, please witness my signature to these deeds.

Lawyer, Puts them before him.

Baron,—Where shall I sign?

Lawyer,—*Points out the place. The Notary and Clerks stand round the table looking at the Baron signing the papers. When the Baron has finished the Clerks sign as witnesses.*

Baron to Notary,—I acknowledge this to be my act and deed. Please put the proper certificate to each deed.

(*While the Notary is doing this Baron rings.*)

Baron, to Servant,—My compliments to Mademoiselle De Plata.— Ask her to please come here.

Exit Servant.

Notary, hands deeds to Lawyer; he looks at them; seeing they are correct he hands them to the Baron.

Lawyer,—They are completed ; all you have to do is to deliver each one to the lady.

Enter INEZ.

Inez (to the Baron,)—I trust you feel better to-day.

Baron,—Thank you, much stronger.

Inez,—Did you rest well last night?

Baron,—Better than since I had that attack on the steamer.

Inez,—Are you not taxing yourself too much ? Are these professional people ? Had you not better leave business to your agents until you are entirely well?

Baron,—I have some papers to give you. I sent for you for that purpose. Gentlemen, permit me to introduce to you, Miss Inez De Plata of New York, the party of the second part in these deeds, which you saw me execute, and which I now deliver to her.

(*Hands Inez the deeds—she takes them, listlessly—sits down in the chair the lawyer has risen from*).

Baron. I thank you, gentlemen.—May I ask you to retire for a short time ?

Exit All, except Baron and Inez.

They are sitting at the table opposite each other.

Inez.—(*Holding the deeds*),—I suppose these are my contracts. (I will read them to-night.) But now tell me when shall we leave for the

Continent. You must not think that I am not sorry to see you ill.—Indeed I am. But I am impatient to be doing something; to be at work. To—to—come out; to sing, and have you taking money in, instead of paying it out—out—always out.

Baron, — (*Is all this time looking at her with wonder studying her.*)

Baron,—Ambitious.

Inez,—(*Rises—walks up and down, getting more and more excited. Baron putting the questions to draw out her real character, which is an enigma to him.*)

Baron,—Would rather rule than serve?

Inez,—Serve? me serve? I am American born, and the equal of any.

Baron,—Had rather rule?

Inez,—Aye! and I will rule. Put me on the platform you promised, and I will show you then whether I'll rule, or not.

Baron,—I will do what I promised.

Inez,—Then put me there. Put me behind the footlights. Fill the house from pit to dome with kings and princes, with statesmen and with warriors, with beauty, fashion, and with wealth. Crowd all the world therein. Then leave me upon that stage alone. And I, girl that I am, I will rule them all. Their proud necks shall bend before me, their breathing stop, their pulses quicker beat, and when the last note, like perfume mingles in the air, spontaneous, and with loudest shouts they to their feet shall spring to honor her that rules them.

Baron,—But you cannot do this without money.

Inez,—But you cannot do that with money.

Baron,—I do not doubt your power, but great though your powers be, without money they never can be heard. Like cannon, without powder, so are talents without money.

Inez,—Then use your money so as to put me where I can be heard, and I will make a noise a world shall hear.

Baron,—This illness I could not help. I did not intend to tell you how serious it is. But now I see I must. I have heart disease; and at any minute I may be extinguished, like gas at opera.

Inez (aside),—Heart disease? Die? If he should, what would be—

come of me?—Pardon me, indeed, I am very sorry—very sorry,—if you will let me I will nurse you myself.

Baron,—Perhaps you shall until I am better, or die.

Inez,—Oh ! do not speak of dying. I will nurse you so carefully if you will let me. Say I may ?

Baron,—Would that be proper ?

Inez,—Proper ?

Baron,—What would the world say—?

Inez,—The world !—What care I what it says ?

Baron,—You should care, for idle tongues move fast and false. Slander loves to sprinkle its vilest poisons on the stage.

Inez,—I have no time to think of that. My life is pure, my object good. Let the buzzards on the carrion feast. They cannot harm me.

Baron,—They would ruin you in your profession.

Inez,—Then what am I to do? I cannot let you die. If you should how am I to reach that platform you promised to place me on.

Baron,—I will show you how to reach it.

Inez,—How ?

Baron,—The first thing is to place the means at your command. Poverty is like a thick fog, it keeps the brightest light from shining.

Inez,—But lightning can pierce and scatter even a fog.

Baron,—Only for an instant.

Inez,—If I am poor I can make riches for you and me. Take me where my light can be seen, and leave rest to me.

Baron,—And for that purpose, take this money, (*hands her a roll of bills*). They do not take up much room.

Inez,—(*takes them listlessly*), How much is here ?

Baron,—About fifty thousand pounds.

Inez,—Fifty thousand pounds. (*Drops the money on the table.*)

Baron,—Take them, they are yours.

Inez,—For what ?

Baron,—To help to support the platform.

Inez,—Why not give it to your agent ?

Baron,—I have nothing to do with the Opera. That money is for you.

Inez,—What, are you not an opera manager ? Did you not engage me to sing in opera ?   Are not these papers (*pointing to the deeds*) my contracts ?

Baron,—Opera ? All I ever had to do with the opera, was to buy a box. I am the Baron Engaltare. These papers are conveyances to you of property worth about five millions of pounds.

Inez,—Five millions of pounds, to me ?

Baron,—Yes.

Inez,—That wealth mine—given by you ?

Baron,—Yes.

Inez,—Then you are a near relation ?

Baron,—I am not.

Inez,—Are you mad, or am I ?

Baron,—We are both perfectly sane. Can I not do what pleases me with my own ?

Inez,—(*aside*). Not an opera manager, not a relation. What is the meaning of all this ? A baron bringing me to Europe—giving me millions —what for ?

Baron,—(*takes the money from the table and hands it to her again*). Do me the favor to accept this.

Inez,—I will not touch one penny of it.

Baron,—Do not be so excited ! Please hear me.

Inez,—Not one word now ! (*rings—furiously*).

Enter Dennis.

(*Pointing to Dennis*),—Would you believe that man ?

Baron,—Implicitly.

Inez,—(*to Dennis*), Look at me—who am I ?

Dennis,—(*aside*), Be the powers, she's mad.

Inez,—Why don't you speak—who am I ?

Dennis,—Why you're my mistress of course,—

Inez,—(*aside*), He does not know me—

(*She puts on the little shawl she had on when first seen in the garret*) Dennis, who am I now ?

Dennis,—Blessed Virgin ! But you're the girl the ould Italian raised —

Inez,—How long have you known me ?

Dennis,—Since you were so—year-old. (*Holding his hand about as high as his hip from the floor.*)

Inez,—Now tell that man there (*points to Baron*) if you ever knew, or heard aught of wrong of me—

Dennis,—Wrong of you?—Niver! A truer, better girl never lived than you. I'd knock the teeth down the throat of the man that would deny it.

Inez,—Do you hear him —Do you believe him?

Baron,—Indeed. I do—

Inez,—Did you think that you could buy me?

Baron,—Buy you! Be calm, and hear me.

Inez,—Calm; oh! yes calm. "Heart disease, suddenly die,"—all a part of the some plan.

Baron,—I beg you to hear me.

Inez,—No. But you hear me. You thought "money was power." You had it by millions. You saw me. Your plan was to lure me through love of my profession, through my ambition, to get me away from friends and country, then to dazzle me with your magnificence, and blind me by a gift of millions, appearing before me like Jupiter in a shower of gold. But you know not the girl you thought you could get with money. Me with money?—There take your money and your deeds —(*Takes them from, and dashes them back on the table*). I am poor, but too rich for any man to buy me. I stand here penniless and alone. No, not alone for here is (*points to Dennis*) one honest man before us, and God above us, to see how I scorn and despise your gifts, and you.

Baron,—You would be right to scorn me, if I had such thoughts of you Me, think thus of you, the child of my dead, and dearest friend. I would be a wretch indeed.

Inez,—What meant you then?

Baron,—I loved your father, he and I were classmates—

Inez,—Loved my father. You knew my father?

Baron,—Knew him and loved him without ceasing from the day when we first met in college. Twenty-three years ago, your father emigrated to America, after that I lost all tidings of him. When I inherited my present wealth and title, I went to New York to find the friend of my youth, and share with him all I possessed. Instead of him, I found his grave. His orphan girl was singing in a little chapel. I wept o'er one, but rejoiced to find his child was left to take the wealth I intended for him.

Inez,—(*weeping*), Forgive me—

Baron,—I saw Father Cregan. I told the good priest all. He and I thought what I have done was the best way to bring you from that little choir, to station and to wealth

Inez,—I want them not.

Baron,—And as I knew that my life might at any minute end, to elevate you as high as in me lay, by leaving you that which is more than wealth, or title—the name of an honored and respected wife.

Inez,—Wife?

Baron,—Yes, by making you my wife, which I do most desire, and entreat you to let me do, and thus add to your happy life, wealth, and title.

Inez,—And you thought your wealth and title would bring great happiness to me?

Baron,—I hoped so. I trust so.

Inez,—And at the cost of losing my profession, shattering my hopes and my whole life's ambition, burying the talents God gave me, making me the holder of your bounty, the bearer of obligations thrust upon me, cutting the wings I hope to fly so high upon, trammeling my freedom, changing my whole life, making me instead of the proud free girl I was, a woman, whose whole end must be to please the man that made her his wife and a Baroness. These were the great benefits you were to give me. Say the cruel, cruel wrongs you would do me.

Baron,—I may have erred, my sole aim then, and now, is to advance, protect, and provide for the child of my dead friend.

Inez,—I do believe you.

Baron,—Then be my wife. A clergyman is in waiting. I have had a special license obtained, and only wait your answer—

Inez,—I want to think, this is all so sudden.

Baron,—Most solemnly, I tell you that, I have spoken the truth—I beg you be my wife, most likely before an hour shall pass, I shall have left this world.—Be now my wife. I then can speedier, happier fly to meet your father. And when I meet him it will rejoice him to hear, and me to say, that I left his child my name, my title and my wealth—

Inez,—Well be it so, but only on this condition. That until I love you—(and that I do not now—) I will never be more of wife to you, than the law doth make me.

Baron,—I am content, the sooner the ceremony is over the better, shall I call them?

Inez,—Yes.

Baron,—*(rings).*

Enter Dennis.

Tell the cleryman, and those waiting in the parlor to come up—
(Exit Dennis).

Enter, Dennis, Clergyman, Lawyer, Notary, Clerk, and others.

Baron,—*rising,* I have called you to witness my marriage with this lady, the daughter of my dearest friend. Mademoiselle are you ready?

Inez, —I am, *(Gives him her hand—)* Dennis, stay close by me.

Episcopal Clergyman, (standing in front of them)

Clergyman—Where is the license?

Lawyer,—*(Hands license to him —Clergyman. Looks at it, seeing it is correct—puts it in the breast of his gown).*

(The marriage proceeds in pantomime—then the Clergyman looking round says.) "Who giveth this woman to be married to this man"?

All are silent.

Inez, —Dennis, I have none this day to do a kinsman's duty. Take thou the place of him that death has taken from me.

Clergyman,—"Who giveth this woman to be married to this man."

Dennis,—I do and proud am I to do it.

(Marriage proceeds in pantomime.)

Clergyman,—"Those that God has joined together let no man put asunder."

(Raises his hands. Benediction in pantomine.)

Baroness, allow me to wish you a happy wedded life.

Inez,—*(sinks in a chair—as if trying to see if she was dreaming.)*

Baron,—*to Lawyer)* Quick, fill up the blank in my will, as I dreat.

Lawyer,—*(takes the will, is preparing to write. Looks at the Baron)*

Baron,—Write—My honored and beloved wife—Inez the Baroness Engaltaro *(Lawyer writes—)* Quick! Quick! Let me sign it—

(Signs the will—Notary and the two Clerks standing round the table witnessing the) (Baron, signing) Gentlemen *(to the Notary and clerks)* I declare this to be my last will and testament. That is my hand and seal,

please witness this my will for me. (*The Notary and two Clerks sign their names to the will—The Lawyer hands the will to the Baron.*)

(*The Baron holding the will falls back in his chair*), Baroness (*she starts*), Inez (*she rises,*) Baron (*gasping—hands her the will,*) my wife (*gasps*) God shield you (*gasps.*) (*falls back in the chair—Dies--*)

Inez—Help! Help! He has fainted.

Lawyer,—Baroness, he is dead.

Inez,—Not dead--Not dead, Oh !

Faints, and is caught by Dennis.

End Scene I.   Act II.

INEZ.

Act II. Scene II. *The same room in the hotel that the Baron died in.*

Discovering LAWYER CUMMINGS, sitting at a table, DENNIS, standing near him.

Dennis,—When is he to be buried, sir?

Lawyer,—We are only waiting for the Spanish Consul.

Dennis,—Had he any relations, Sir?

Lawyer,—Not to my knowledge.

Dennis,—If he had would that hurt my lady?

Lawyer,—Not a particle.

Dennis,—So my lady is safe anyway?

Lawyer,—Quite so.

Dennis,—No relation can bother the property?

Lawyer,—But he had no relations.

Dennis,—But if he had, sir?

Lawyer, —It would make no difference. She holds some of the property by deed vesting it in her prior to the marriage. The rest she takes by last will and testament.

Raps at the door.

Lawyer,—See who that is.

Dennis,—[*Opens the door. Receives a salver from a hotel Servant; presents the salver to Lawyer he takes visiting card from the salver.*

Lawyer,—It is the Spanish Consul. I will go down and see him.

Lawyer, Exits.

Dennis, [*talking to himself*],—Me poor lady, what will she do now? Go back on the stage? Arrah! Dinnis what are you thinking of? Is it the likes of her, an she a baroness, go on the Varieties? (Not but there's as good women there as anywhere, and better; for they work harder; some of them supporting their husbands and their children; some their fathers and mothers—and they too ould to work for themselves); I knew one. Oh! stop your varieties. Dinnis, sir—Do you think she'd iver go anywhere now but on the opera, where they play and sing that outlandish tongue the ould Italian taught her in the garret at home. Arrah? an why did'nt he lave me tache her Irish? why should'nt she larn it now? She can larn anything with that head of hers, she'd larn Irish 'fore Christmas. And then with that voice of hers, Oh! Mother of Moses, would'nt she bate all their operas, singing Irish. Dinnis, sir—You're a fool! Who'd go to hear her sing Irish? Who? The avenues, be Gorra? that's who—besides a slice of Brooklyn, Jersey, Harlem, and many a one from up, and down-town.—That's who would go to hear her sing Irish—

Dinnis—Sir—suppose you set up for a manager—(just to lighten her heart of this sorrow) sure she'll never be free of the trouble 'till she's singing agin! Set up for a manager to plase her. Larn her the rale ould Irish yourself. Rent Gilmore's Garden, thin with electrical lights, and big posters, and letters a foot long, stuck all over town, and on the finces and rocks across the river as far as Philadelphia, and on the other side out by the Park, and down to Coney Island, rading like this:—

[*Drawing with his finger in the air, each imaginary line, as he reads it. Standing, C. fronting the audience.*]

Trimindious Success

of the grate

-——MISS BOUROUGH——

a legitimate disendant of

-——BRIAN BOUROUGH——

and the only rale one of the kind in the world.—

Under the management of
GENERAL DINNIS MULLONEY,
at
Gilmore's Garden,
in a ginuine Irish Opera,
—called—

Erin wili get her own again.
None but the ould Irish aristocracy admitted to the Boxes.
Tickets $5.00.
Divil a less, for they're all taken-
(There's a manager's janius for you. "The ould Irish aristocracy."
That one line will put every one of the women, pestering the life out of
the ould man, for the price of one of thim boxes.)
Seats in chairs, 50 Cents.
Seates without chairs, 25 Cents.
Gineral admittance. Go as you plaze. (That manes—with, or without coats)
—10 Cents.-

There's a bill for you   There's the thing to fill the Garden, and take
in the money. Be the powers but I'd spend it in the country I got it
from—an that's more than a Chiniman does. Dinnis—Sir—You're a grate
man, that head of yours is wonderful; 't wil be the making of you yet.
And wo'nt she smile again, when she's back on the stage, the darling?

Enter Lawyer, and sits down.

Lawyer,--Come here, Dennis, and listen carefully to what I tell
you--

Dennis,—Yes, sir.

Lawyer,—Dennis, I am going to trust you. I believe you are an
honest man.

Dennis,—Well that ain't much to brag of, I had an honest man for
a father before me, and he's in Ireland now, living comfortible in his
ould age; thanks to me lady.

Lawyer,—It is of her I wish to speak. I am afraid there is trouble
in the future for her.

Dennis,—Trouble,—I'd like to see the man that would throw a sha-
dow of trouble on the ground she walks on, much less on her.

Lawyer, -And it is because of your devotedness to her that I am
going to confide in you, so that you may know what are the evils that I
apprehend, and therefore be always near to guard her.

Dennis,—What is it, sir?

Lawyer,—The Spanish Consul has just now told me that he had no-
tified his government of the sudden death of the baron; tendering to carry
out any wishes of the relatives. That he had received an answer. That

there were no relations of the baron alive, unless his sister's child, which if living would be Alfonso the Count Diego; but whether he was alive or not, was not positively known. But it was believed that he had been drowned at sea while [a boy. That upon receiving this answer he had advertised for information of the Count, and offered a reward of—£1,000 to any person who would produce proof to establish that the Count was alive and where he was now.

Dennis,—An I suppose he asked you like a grate American once did, "What are you going to do about it?"

Lawyer,—Exactly.

Dennis,—And what did you say, sir?

Lawyer,—That my client an American lady had married the baron. That he by his last will and testament had left her all his property and made her his executrix. That whether the Count Diego was alive or dead, it could not affect the property.

Dennis,—Oh! then he's a gentleman, sure.

Lawyer,—He then said that the day following the insertion of the advertisement a man called on him, and said that he knew that the Count Diego was alive and that if he was paid the £1000 he would produce the Count in six weeks; that the Count had gone to sea when he was a boy, had been shipwrecked, but escaped, and he knew where he was. That he told the man to call to-day—and that his man would be at his office at 2 o'clock, and asked me what course he should take.

Dennis,—What did you say to that, sir?

Lawyer,—I simply said that he could do what he thought best, but that I did not believe one word of what the man said. That my client would not give him one shilling—

Dennis,—And why should she pay to find a poor relation? There's no sense in that; they always find their rich relations, without much difficulty. If he's alive he'll find her—divil a doubt of it. But what did the Consul say then?

Lawyer,—Only that he should inform the man of what I said—

Dennis,—A gentleman that, every inch of him.

Lawyer,—I fear there is trouble in this. I am positive the Count Diego died while a boy. I think that some sharp, cunning rascal who was thoroughly acquainted with the baron, knowing of his death, and seeing this advertisement conceived the idea of going to the Spanish Consul, telling him that story so as to obtain the £1000, and afterwards to appear himself as the Count Diego, the baron's next of kin, and thus claim the whole property. A well conceived scheme, as infamous as it was cleverly planned.

Dennis.—If iver I lay an eye on him.

Lawyer. - Be quiet, Dennis. You cannot defend your lady and her property from such a plot as that, with violence.

Dennis.—Aye, then, I'd brake the neck of him—what am I to do, sir?

Lawyer.—Be watchful.

Dennis.—Watchful, a bull-dog shan't bate me at that! Watch for her? I'd die for her.

Lawyer.—Do not alarm her by telling her anything of this. If you see anything suspicious, or any one prying into her affairs let me know. In short be always near her.

Dennis.—Yes, an I ll keep me stick handy.

Lawyer.—She may go to Spain to see the baron interred, and settle some business there. If she does, redouble your watchfulness, and advise me of anything that you think unusual. Do you promise to do this?

Dennis.—I do, and I will on the honor of a man.

Enter INEZ,—*in Widow's Weeds.*

The LAWYER *puts a chair for her.*

Inez.—You are very kind. When will he be buried?

Lawyer.—There will be services at the chapel this morning. Then the body will be sent to Spain, to be placed in the family tomb.

Inez.—Am I to go?

Lawyer.—Not unless you desire it.

Inez.—I do.

Lawyer.—Well, as you prefer.

Inez.—Where is he now?

Lawyer.—In the next room. Do you wish to see him?

Inez.—Presently. (*Weeps*).

Lawyer (*Hands* INEZ *a photograph of the* BARON),—When we were putting his things away, I saw this; thinking you would like to have it I kept it out for you.

Inez,—Thank you; (*looking at it*). It is very, very like him. (*Weeping,*) Oh! Baron, why did I not understand you sooner? I did not love you; but now I almost do; Oh! Baron, what shall your widow do?—How shall she act? Why did you leave her so soon? Oh! Baron, Baron, I am so wretched!

Dennis,—My lady, do not take it so hard! Don't cry!

Inez,—Tears? These are not tears!

Lawyer,—He is happy. He was a good man. He loved your father. Therefore he has left you all his wealth.

Inez,—It is that wealth which bows me down; that changes me from what I was, to what I am. It oppresses me. I do not knw what to do with it.

Lawyer,—You can do good with it.

Inez,—And I will. But how?

Lawyer,—There are many ways.

Inez,—You had his confidence; now you have mine. You knew him well, his plans, his views, tell me, what would he have done with it if he had not found me? What would he have done?

Lawyer,—I do not know.

Inez, (*to the photograph*),—Baron, you found me poor. You made me rich, but your riches weigh me down, my spirits are all gone,—my ambition checked. I want to be myself again, but I cannot. Baron, what shall I do with it? Baron, what would you have me do with it?

Dennis,—She's going crazy. God pity her.

Inez,—Oh! that I was back in my garret again!

Lawyer,—God will tell you in his own good time, what use to make of it.

Inez, (*to the photograph*),—You were a good man. Forgive me for ever speaking harshly to you. But oh! I could not help it. I thought you were going to put me on a different stage than this.

Dennis,—Sit down, my lady.

Inez,—Sit down? I must move.—Act,—lo,—anything but be still.—Is this me? where now are all my hopes, where now my aspirations, where the longing for the day to come that was to try my powers, and make my fame? Where that confidence in myself that knew no doubt, or hesitation? Where the engrossing thoughts that once possessed me? All,—all,—are gone. And what is left of me? Nothing but this body, this flesh and bone ;—that's all. My very name is changed :—no one calls me INEZ now,—but the baroness :—and who is she? I scarcely know her. INEZ, was myself. Now I am new in station—new in name. Oh! that I was INEZ again !

Lawyer,—Baroness, I beg you, try and compose yourself. They are going to close the casket. Do you wish to see him before 'tis done.

Inez,—Yes, I'll go and see him. See him for the last time.

Lawyer,—Shall I go with you, or do you wish to see him alone?

Inez, –Alone. I'll go alone. I am alone.

(*Curtain drawn back, showing a Coffin,* INEZ *moving towards the casket.*)

MUSIC.—END OF SCENE II. ACT II.

Act II.

Scene II. ' *Woods in Spain on the outskirts of the City.*

Enter Count Diego.

Count Diego (*looking around*), Yes, this is the place ; there is the big tree ; it is as secluded here as if there was not a house within a thousand miles. Who would think a great city is within a gun shot of this deserted wood? Many a time when I played truant have I hid here until school was out. It will serve me now for another purpose. No danger of being heard here. Few come here in day light and none at night. I wish that ruffian would come. It must be past the hour I told him, or may be it is my impatience that overreaches time. No wonder it does. Mine is a game where the stakes outweigh those of Baden-Baden, my life, if lost, prodigious, wealth if won. Should I lose, —well, who cares ? I have day to die ; it can only shorten the days at the worst. But if I win the days will then be filled with power and all the homage that the world to the rich man cringing brings (*whistle outside*). That's the signal now to answer.

[*Takes a whistle out of his pocket, whistles twice which is returned outside. Then Count Diego whistles once*]

Enter Juan De Plata.

De Plata,—Here I am.

Count,—You should have been here before.

De Plata,—Wait until you own me, before you say should. What do you want with me ?

*Count,—*To do me a service for which I will pay you well.

*De Plata,—*That's more like it. What's the job and how much? Though I don't want to go back where I have been the last fourteen years, if you'll give enough for the risk I'll try to serve you. But I want no fooling. Money down, that's me! Now out with it plain!— What's the job? Where's the money? I don't know you, and you don't know me. Money down,—short acquaintance; I come, you go; do your business, have the money in my pocket; things settled, no need of meeting again, part good friends,—cash and no credit. I'm done,—cash—! [*Holding out his hands*]

*Count,—*Not so fast, my friend; I never pay until the goods are delivered.

*De Plata,—*Then what did you come to me for? I don't sell on credit; I don't know you.

*Count,—*But I know you, so wait until I talk a little. You have done the most of it since you came.

*De Plata—*Go ahead!

*Count,—*You came out of prison about two weeks ago, after serving fourteen years for killing the mate of the ship you were on while on the voyage from America here. You got fourteen years of convict life for that "job". I'll pay you better than that You see when you did a 'job" for yourself it didn't yield much. Moral,—Don't go again into business for yourself; hire out,—you'll do better!

*De Plata,—*Who asked you for your advice?

*Count,—*Don't interrupt me, or be hasty! We'll understand each other better.

*De Plata,—*You're too smooth for my liking. Say what you want, or I'm going.

Count,— Going? Not till I'm done with you!

[*Takes out a whistle; gives a long quivering whistle.*]

Ruffians appear instantly at each wing.

De Plata looks around; sees he is surrounded by men and cannot escape.

I thought you were one of the secret police. But you can't hurt me; I served my time out.

*Count,—*You mistake again, and you're not going until I say so. Do you suppose I'd trust you here, to let you go until I told you?

To the ruffians who are at the entrances on each side,—

Come here; take a good look at this man!

[*They all surround De Plata; peer in his face; look at him from head to foot.*]

*Count Diego,—*Follow this man! [*pointing to De Plata*] night and day; never let him be out of your sight one instant. If you see him going near the police, or anywhere likely for him to squeal, cut his throat. Don't let him out of this wood until I give you the signal. When I do follow him as close as his own hair. Now go where you came from, and wait for the signal Go.

Ruffians exit.

Count Diego lights a segar.

So you "don't give credit?" You credited me with too little sense to suppose that I'd trust you. No, my cautious friend, I don't trust you, but you shall work for me, and on credit too. When your "job" is done I'll pay you gold enough to fill your hat; you shall not grumble at the pay. I know you want to go back to America.

*De Plata,—*How do you know that?

*Count,—*Never mind now! I know it. Now do what I tell you, and you shall go there with money enough to live without ever doing a "job" again. You'll find me a good cash customer. I cannot get the gold to pay you until you do the work for me. But when you do you shall have it.

*De Plata,—*Suppose I refuse, what then ?

*Count,—*Then you're a dead man. A corpse or two in these woods makes little difference. I rather think it would improve the scenery—our friends just left are of the same opinion. You forget what I told them.

*De Plata (aside),—*I see no way out of this. I suppose I'll have to kill, or be killed. If I could only get that whistle.

*Count (taking out the whistle),—*I'm waiting for your answer. Do you agree to do whatever I tell you, or forfeit your life ?

*De Plata,—*Of course I do since I have to—(*Snatches the whistle* *out of the* Count's *hands*), No I don't. I have changed my mind--why don't you whistle now for your canaries--

(*Count—Takes another whistle out of his vest pocket, quickly—and whistles two sharp notes--*

Suddenly the ruffians are back with their knives in their hands--)

Count Diego (*with a mocking laugh*),—You see I carry two. I did whistle as you requested. (*To the ruffians*) Go back!—*Exit Ruffians*—Now what do you say? Do you accept? Will you obey me?

De Plata,—I suppose, I must.

Count,—Will you?

De Plata (*sullenly*),—Yes.

Count,—There is an American woman stopping at one of the hotels here. I want you to send her to heaven, she is too good for earth. Get her a through ticket with your stiletto.

De Plata,—How shall I know her?

Count,—She shall be pointed out to you. Her room is the one on the first floor, with a window fronting the street.

De Plata,—Killing should always be avoided if possible--what do you want to kill her for? Is it to rob the room?

Count,—What's that to you?

De Plata,—Well if you want your work done clean, how am I going to do it in the dark? I don't want the job, but you make me. Better get some other fellow who won't bother you with questions—

Count,—No, you must do it,—I have gone too far with you. You must not touch anything in that room. When she's gone it will all be mine—That's the way I get the money to pay you.

De Plata,—Who is she?

Count,—The Baroness Eugaltare.

De Plata,—I thought you said she was an American—

Count,—And so she is. The Baron went to America with the romantic idea of finding a college chum of his, a good for nothing rascal called Juan De Plata.

De Plata, (*starts aside,*)--If he did but know to whom he was talking--

Count,--The fellow was dead but he left a daughter--The Baron brought her to England, and intended coming here.—He sent me on to make preparations for his arrival.--While I was here, he died--The

Consul sent the news here, and enquired for his relations.—I knew he had none, so I returned. Went to the Consul intending to claim his property, and was referred to a lawyer.—There I found the baron had married an American woman, and died in a few moments—leaving her all his property, and that she had come here with the body, to have him buried—I hurried back. I have powerful friends—no matter how I got them—I have them—when she is out of the way—they will have the whole thing set aside and I declared to be the Count Diego and as such get all he left as his nearest relation—Do you see now why you must finish her without robbing her?

De Plata,—Let me think.—Is there no other way?

Count,—No,—I tell you, no—she is the daughter of that fellow that died—

De Plata,—Of who?

Count,—Of Juan De Plata. Did'nt I tell you he married her, a few minutes before he died?—(De Plata *puts his hand on his knife*), if you don't kill her! Those who use me, will have it done. I am only their tool—to reach the Baron's property, of course, they make me the Count Diego and give me half. What's the matter with you?

De Plata,—Nothing, except I'm chilled with cold, and the scare your pets outside there gave me.

Count,—Take a drink of that (*hands him a flask*; *De Plata drinks*). —Now do what I tell you, and you are safe, neither you nor I can stop, I am more in their power, than you are in mine. Those fellows out there, who watch you—watch me—so the sooner we finish this by putting her out of the way, and having me made the Count Diego, the sooner we both get the money and save our own lives.

De Plata,—There's where you are wrong, the sooner she is dead, the sooner you will be killed after they have made you the Count.—You would not trust me. Do you think they'll let you live with their secret or me either? Mark my words, after you get all the property as the Count Diego you'll die suddenly (*aside—I must save her life.*)

Count,—I must run that risk, it is the only way.

De Plata,—If you'll pay me well I'll tell you how to get all the property, save yourself, and get her besides. Pay me well, and I'll show you, and wait for the money until you get it.

Count,—Tell me and I will.

De Plata,— Marry her, don't you see? Marry her, you get it all as her husband, without any thanks to them.

Count,—That's worth considering. That would give it all to me; yes and her too, (until I have done with her.) I'll think over it. Now recollect: If you even breathe to yourself one word of what I told you, you are a dead man. From this minute you are under the eyes of those whose knives are as sharp as their consciences are blunt. Meet me to—morrow at the same place. Now you can go 'till then. (*Whistles two short sharp notes, and one long note. Ruffians appear at the wings.*) *To Ruffians,*—Let him go, but never beyond your sight!

Exit De Plata,—*followed by the others.*

Count,—Marry her? There's a good deal in that advice. I hate her, yet I would give much to have her. She's beautiful, but that spirit of hers,—oh! I'd break her neck in three weeks. But would she marry me? Why of course, if she sees she'll lose her lately gotten title and riches unless she does. A singing girl give up them? She's not such a fool. Marry her? I'll think of it.

END OF SCENE III.

Act II. Scene IV.

Inez's room in a hotel in Spain. Inez *seated.*

Inez,—I wish I was out of this place. I feel oppressed. I cannot sleep at night. The very air is heavy. Why should I stay here longer? The baron is in his last resting place, in that cold, cold tomb. That tomb has left its chill upon me, its icy chill. I wish I had not seen that abode of death. It will stand photographed on my brain forever. It seemed to me as I stood between the rows of those coffined knights and dames, as though they hated me, and colder in their shrouds got because I a stranger held their title and their gold. Perhaps they would have liked me better if they knew how little I prize it. I had rather be Inez, living as I was, and when dead to be laid within the breast of my mother earth; in my own free land, there beneath its daisies nestled, until the trumpet shall sound to bring its dead flowers and me to immortal life, than to live here a baroness, and dying molder in that grand but awful tomb. I am frozen with dread of unknown ills; I feel that I am surrounded by evils that I cannot see. I cannot bear this, I will leave here. Pshaw! Am I so nervous grown that I suffer from imagination? This comes from thinking, thinking, thinking, when I should be doing, doing, doing.—

—*Rises in nervous petulance,*—The whole of it is, the sooner I get away the sooner I'll feel better, and the sooner I dismiss from my mind the load of responsibility this sudden possession of enormous wealth has placed upon it, the sooner I will feel like myself.

*—Sits—meditating,—*I must have some one to manage it for me. But who can I get, and who can I trust? I know but three men I would trust. First, there is the baron's lawyer, but he's too busy with law. Second, there is Father Cregan, the dear old man; he knows more of heaven than of earth. Third, Dennis—why I might as well give Dennis my guitar to tune. Good, honest Dennis! Why he is so troubled with his own money, that he gives me his wages to keep. Who can I trust? Oh! happy thought! My country, I'll trust it all to you!—In your bonds it will be safe from fire and from thieves, in your bonds it will yearly bear good fruit. There I will plant this golden tree, and its rich fruit shall go through channels safe and sure. To elevate my sisters, to find homes for the sick and suffering of my sex, to teach them the means of selfsupport, advancing them in all that's good and defending them from harm.

I will write and direct the baron's lawyer to have this done without delay—

May heaven bless the undertaking!

— Writes—seals the Letter.—Rings.—

There, that is done. Now I feel a great deal better, ever so much better.

Enter DENNIS.

(*To Dennis*),—I want this letter to go to London by the first mail. It is important; now be sure that it goes by the first mail.

*Dennis,—*Yes, my lady, but to be sure that it does go, I'll take it myself to the English Consul and get him to send it with his letters. Thin it will go, safe and sound. The baron's lawyer tould me always to do that with important letters. I'll go at once and do it. Will you want anything before I go, for 'tis a long way to the Consul's house?

*Inez,—*No, thanks, that is all now.

Exit DENNIS.

Did I ever think that having so much money would make me miserable, and that I would be doing my best to get clear of it by giving it to others?

(*Noise outside as if trying to open the window.*) INEZ *starts,* —What noise was that? All this has made me nervous! I had stronger nerves in my little garret room.

Noise again. INEZ *starts, then becomes perfectly self-reliant.* That was somebody trying to get in at the window. *Is about to ring.* Dennis is out. *Goes to the trunk, quietly opens it.* Come here, my little friend. *Takes out a revolver.* I want you now that Dennis is gone. *She goes to the table, sits, her left hand on the table supporting her head, her right holding the revolver, under the table. Feigns sleep.*

DE PLATA—*Looks at her through the window, enters, stealthily approaches the table, leaning across it. Looks at* INEZ, *who suddenly rises and points the pistol at his head.*—What do you want?

De Plata,—I am no robber. I mean you no harm.

Inez,—What brings you here?

De Plata,—I have periled my life to come here to speak to you.

Inez,—About what? (*Puts the pistol in her pocket*).

De Plata,—About your father and dangers that surround you.

Inez,—My father? What do you know of my father?

De Plata,—None knew him better than I.

Inez,—You are trying hard to deceive me.

De Plata,—No, on my salvation, no!

Inez,—Go on.

De Plata,—I was in college with your dead husband. He was a noble youth. We loved each other dearly, but we never met, after we graduated, for I went to America after my mother's death—which was about twenty-five years ago.

Inez (aside),—What tale is this?

De Plata,—Day by day I got poorer, and then to add to my misery, I met a young girl as poor as myself, but oh! so beautiful! I married her, she and I existed, and that was all. She died, leaving an infant girl, and me too poor to even bury her. But kind people did. The poor are oftener kinder than the rich.

Inez,—Aye! well I know it. Did you love her?

De Plata,—Indeed, indeed I did.

Inez,—Who was she?

De Plata,—The orphan girl of a musician, she tried to live by teaching music. She had very few pupils and they could pay her but little.

Inez,—Tell me where she lies, and I will plant the earth above her thick with flowers.

De Plata,—I do not know where she lies.

Inez,—Do not know? Why not? did you not see her buried? Why don't you speak?

De Plata,—(*Hiding his face, bending over the table,*) Because I was in jail for beating her while I was drunk.

Inez, —Beating her? Oh! you wretch!

De Plata,- I was so drunk. I did not know what I was doing—

Inez,—Oh! how I hate you!

De Plata,—Oh! do not hate me! I am your father! I came here to save you!

Inez,—You, my father? Save me? You lie, I never came from such a wretch as you! My father is dead!

De Plata, —I wish he was.

Inez,—Great God, is this my father?

De Plata,—Yes, this is your father, and her I told you of was your mother. You were three years old when she died. I never knew until this day why she was taken, and I was left; but I know it now. It was to save you.

Inez,—To save me?

De Plata,—Yes, I see I was kept alive until now, to save you. Listen. After your mother died I was but seldom sober, but I managed to keep you and myself alive. I used to leave you with the old Italian who lived in the next room. He was seldom out, because he was a composer, writing music for songs; that was the way he lived, and little he got for it. He said you were company for him, so he took care of you. One day I was near the wharfs with some Spanish sailors. We all got drunk. What happened next I never knew, except when I awoke. I was out at sea upon a Spanish ship bound for a Spanish port. On the voyage, I struck the mate, I struck too hard, it killed him, they put me in irons,

tried me when I reached the shore.   My life was saved because I did not
strike until I was struck, but as an example to all sailors (so said the
judge) I was imprisoned with hard labor for fourteen years   I was relea-
sed but two weeks since.

Inez,—When free why did you not go with honest men and work ?

De Plata,—Honest men ? what honest men would go with me ? or
who would give the convict work ? I was trying every way to get back to
America to find out if you were alive.

Inez,—What did you do for food and shelter ?

De Plata,—I herded with those who had been convicts like myself,
or would be. It was this or starve.

Inez,—How came you here ? And how came you to know me ? I do
not believe I am your child.

De Plata,—You are my child.   The child I loved in all these years,
and longed once more to see.

Inez,—If this was so, how came you to find, and know me ?   You
had not seen me for fourteen years. I was only five years old when last
you saw me.   This is a tale to get money by working on my feelings.

De Plata,—God knows I tell the truth. Last night while in a cellar
where some of us late convicts burrow, a man approached me, told me
to meet him in three hours in a wood outside of the city, and when I
came he would show me how to make more money than I ever had.   I
did it, what happened when we met is not important. I found myself
in the power of a gang of cutthroats who since then watch me every minute, at the command of the baron's valet.

Inez,—Of who ?

De Plata,—Of the baron's valet, who there stood before me.   He
told me your whole history and wanted me to take your life for gold.

Inez,—Murder me !

De Plata,—He wants you dead. He has those acting with him,
who will have him declared to be the baron's next of kin, who will go
further, decree your marriage void, the will invalid, and give the baron's
property to him. That's why he wanted to hire me to murder you.

Inez,—To have me murdered ?

De Plata,—Yes and me to do it. He little knew he was talking to your father. From him I heard all about my little girl. Oh! God, how I suffered while that man talked to me in that wood. My hand was on my knife to kill the man that wanted to force me to kill my child.--

Inez,--Why did you not kill him, there and then? You would have done it if you had been my father.

De Plata,--I tell you I was going to put my knife in his heart, when I saw that if I did, some one else would be palmed off as the Count Diego instead of this valet, that if I did not pretend to agree I would never leave that wood alive, and some one else would surely assassinate you. This valet is only the tool of mighty people, powerful people!

Inez,--Get me away from here! I'll give you gold enough for every risk you run!

De Plata,--You would be killed before you could leave this town. Their spies are all around.

Inez,--What shall I do? Go on tell me what happened next?

De Plata,--I pretended to agree, I promised to obey him in all things. I was and I am in his power; my life is worth less than yours, and in greater danger. I advised him to marry you, showing him that by marrying you he could save himself, get all your wealth and you. I counseled him to marry you.

Inez,—You say you are my father, and counseled him to marry me?

De Plata,--Yes, and I counsel you to wed him! Wed him, to save your wealth--and life--else they will murder you.

Inez,—Me wed him? Wed that wretch?

De Plata,—Oh! my child, wed him. They are full of power those who use him to get your wealth. I beseech you to do what I tell you--It is the only way to save your life and wealth. It is your father who wants you to save your life by wedding him.--

Inez,--Wed that slimy snake?

De Plata,--Yes, for by so doing you keep his deadly fangs from your fair life. He runs great risk, great risk! He is watched, as well as me, and no one but a man in love would take such a risk as he will take if he marries you.

Inez,—That devil, love me? How do you know this?

De Plata,—Because he said when I told him that he need not kill you but to marry you. That he would think of it, that it was worth considering—that that would give him all your wealth and you until he was done with you.

Inez,—And you heard him say that, and let him live and you, my father? Out of my sight! I abhor you! My God! My God! Can this be my father?

Runs to her trunk, takes out a purse and throws it to him.

(*He lets it drop.*) Take it, take it, I say. (*Reluctantly he picks up the purse.*) Go, there is gold enough to take you from this country and keep you from committing crime. Go, and never let me see your face again. (*Points to the door.*) Go, go, go!

Exits DE PLATA

Oh? My God! this is too much!

END ACT II.

ACT III.

SCENE I. *Spain,—A cellar,—Convicts,—Robbers playing cards,
others lying on the floor, others drinking,—Door with steps leading down
into this Robbers' Den.*

First Robber,—When I was behind the bars.

Second Robber,—Stop that, we all have been there.

Third Robber,—Yes, know it all. Tell us something we don't know,
— something fresher.

Robber enters with sack on his back. Throws it down.

Robber,—There, that's all we got to-night, and hard work at that.
Had to break open two stores and a kitchen to get that. Times are
hard, and people are getting too poor to be robbed.

First Ruffian,—The whole lot ain't worth two ounces! Try a bank,
or a swell's till the next time. No.use of wasting genius on such stuff
as that.

DE PLATA *enters, goes off by himself, sits down dejected.*

First Ruffian [to De Plata],—What's the matter? Got the repent-
ance, and only two weeks out? Want to go back to the quarries? Take a
pull at this, and you'll feel better. [*Hands him a bottle.*]

De Plata (drinks, hands back the bottle,)—Good fellow!

Enter COUNT DIEGO.

Count goes up to De Plata, and says in low voice, —Have you finished her?

De Plata,—No.

Count, — Why?

De Plata,—My heart failed me; I can't.

Count,—I told you I had given up the idea of marrying her. The last thing I told you was to make your knife transfer the property to me by cutting her —[*Motions across his throat*].

De Plata,—I can't do it.

Count,—Chicken-hearted! Any of these fellows here would do it for a tenth of what I am going to give you.

De Plata,—No, they couldn't. That Irishman is always near her.

Count,—Pshaw! Wait till she goes to bed, get in through the window, a slash with a sharp knife, and she's in heaven. The gold is yours, and you on your way back to America.

De Plata,—It can't be done. Dennis puts a cot across her door, and sleeps on it every night. To get into her room a man would have to move Dennis and his cot before he could open the door.

Count,—Then find some other way.

De Plata,—I don't know how.

Count,—You don't know how? You're a pretty strawberry and cream, chap! You don't know how? What pious people educated you? You don't know how?

De Plata,—And I don't.

Count,—And you shall, and do it too! Do you suppose that after my disclosing to you my plans I'm going to let you off now? You forget what happened in the woods? Go this night, and let not the sun see her alive, or—

*De Plata—Rising,—*Or? Finish your words.

Count,—Or, I'll finish you—

De Plata,—I won't touch a hair of her head, but you shall not leave here alive. You're not in the woods now with your gang to come when you whistle; you're here; here among my chums. My Count, valet, you forget where you are: You had your palls 'round you last time—I have mine now.

Count,—*Derisively laughs,*—Ha! Ha! Ha! (*Takes out a segar, lights it.*) Call your "palls,"—we'll see if they will do what you tell them Once for all—will you kill her?

De Plata,—No—But I'll send you where you wished her to go. (*To the* RUFFIANS) Men, here is a spy—(RUFFIANS *all draw their knives and spring towards the* COUNT). This fellow is one of the secret police, he has been trying to bribe me to sell you; offered me fifty doubloons to squeal on you. Kill him, and throw him in the river.

The RUFFIANS *make a dash at the* COUNT *with their knives.* COUNT *makes a sign with his hand.—The instant he makes the sign the* RUF-FIANS *all drop their knives. Bow their heads. Standing like statues before him.* DE PLATA *looking at them in wonder, and they at him with fear.—*

Count,—You see what a mistake you were making. Pick up your knives!—(*They do it*)—Now bind that lying hound.—(*Pointing to* DE PLATA.—*The* RUFFIANS *seize* DE PLATA *and tie him,*) Search him!—(*They search him, and find* INEZ'S *purse, showing it to the* COUNT.)—

First Ruffian,—Here is a purse with the word INEZ engraved on the rings—

Count,—Damnation! Divide the gold among you. Give me the purse! Those whose sign you saw, ordered that man to do what they wanted. He swore he would.—But instead of doing it he betrays their secrets, and tries to have you kill me. I am their officer. You know they open and shut prison doors?

First Ruffian,—We know it, tell us what to do, and we'll do it.

All the Ruffians,—We'll do it.

Count,—Get a rope, hang the dog!

De Plata,—One minute to make one prayer.

Count,—I give you two minutes. (*Takes out his watch.*)

De Plata, kneeling—while a RUFFIAN *puts a rope 'round his neck, prays with his tied hands lifted up,—*Oh! God forgive me all I ever did. This man wanted me to kill my own child—will you who are a just God let him murder me, because I would not murder my own child?

Count,—Your child? Is she your child?

De Plata,—She is.

Count,—I don't believe it. What is your name?

De Plata,—Juan De Plata.

Count,—You lie, you dog.—You lie!

De Plata,—Untie me, let me write to her—read the letter, and send it to her yourself—you can get her answer in less time than an hour, and you'll see if I lie —

Count,—Untie him. (*The* CONVICTS *do it.*)—Now go to that table.

One of you go and get pen and ink. I want him to write a letter. (DE
PLATA *walks towards the table, gets near it —and suddenly runs up the
steps to escape. He is on the steps, when the* COUNT *draws a pistol, aims,
fires.* DE PLATA *reels on to the floor—staggers, and falls dead*) She
ought to pay me for that. *The door is burst open.* COUNT *escapes
through a trap.* SOLDIERS —*fill the doorway—and aim their muskets at
the* CONVICTS. *The* CONVICTS *cowering down under the muskets.*

End,

SCENE I.

Act III. Scene II.

Reception room.   Same hotel in Spain.

_____

Count Diego—*Enters—Followed by a hotel* Servant, *puts down his hat, takes out a visiting card, handing it to the* Servant.

For the Baroness Engaltaro.

*Exit—*Servant.

Count,—Will she do what I wish ? I can't have her put out of the way, as I intended. She's on her guard against that. That cursed convict must have told her. She must either marry me, or—well, never mind that now. The first thing is to see if she will marry me. I don't think she'll refuse when she knows what it will cost her to refuse me. But I'll first try and coax her—all women are either won by praise, or fooling. They think they are wronged if a man don't lie to them, though they know he's lying, when he swears he thinks that she is an angel ; that he loves her; so he can't live without her. She's no exception, I should judge, like all her sex, she wants to get either riches, or love; she has riches. I'll show her I adore her, love her to distraction, and wind up by showing her, unless she takes the man that adores her, she will lose all her newly found wealth and— —

*Enter—*Inez.

Count.—Baroness, I have the honor of calling on you to—

Inez,—What is your business. I must be excused from anything but important business.

Count,—It is very important business, or I would not have called.

Inez,—Be seated, and let me hear it.

Count,—You are a lady of great ability and—

Inez,—Your business, and please be explicit.

Count,—Since you command it,—well perhaps it is best to be "explicit." I came here under a fictitious name. Had I sent you my true name you might not have seen me. You see I am changed in appearance, as well as name, since you don't recognize me.

Inez,—I never saw you in my life,—what is your motive for coming to me?

Count,—My motive is to see a woman I adore, and to save her life—

Inez,—Leave off such language? To save me—what can you know of me?

Count,—I know your whole history from your birth and life in the garrets of New York, to this hour. I know that unless you do what I tell you you will be in your grave before sixty days are gone by.

Inez,—(*Rises to go.*) – Sir!

Count,—Wait and hear me. You need not be afraid of me.

Inez,—Afraid of you?—(*Derisively,*)—Afraid of you?

Count,—Then hear me, and afterwards do what you wish.

Inez,—Be brief then.

Count,—I was in America when the Baron was looking for your father. You see I talk like an Englishman.

Inez,—I'd understand you better if you would act like an Englishman. Be as blunt, and honest as one — —

Count,—I will be blunt enough to please you, I hope. Well, I first saw you in the choir in New York. I heard you pour forth a flood of melody like a stream of music running out from heaven's gateway. Every day after I watched you for the Baron and myself.

Inez,—For the baron, and yourself?

Count,—Yes for him, to report your daily life, for myself to feed the passion that your beauty woke within me.

Inez—(*rises,*)—Another word like that and I leave the room. Who are you?

Count,—Alphonso, the Count Diego, the baron's next of kin and heir at law.

Inez,—Out, you lying imposter, or I'll hand you over to the police

—you the Count Diego? I know you now—you were the baron's valet.
How dare you come into my presence?

Count,—You are not in America now. You're in Spain. If you hear
me, it may save you trouble.

Inez,—Hear you? You who hired a convict to kill me? Come, do it
yourself. (*Draws a stiletto*)—Why don't you do it now? If I am in Spain
I can defend myself from hearing words of love from such a slimy reptile
as you are.

Count,—I like that—magnificent. Take your choice—marry me or—

Inez,—Or what—?

Count,—Or be arrested and tried for conspiracy—poisoning and ob-
taining in that way the baron's property. If this charge is made against
you by me you will be garrotted, I will be declared to be entitled to the
property and will take it all as next of kin.

Inez,—So failing in having me killed by your bravo you would try
the law as a cheaper, safer assassin. You forget no one would believe it.

Count,—Any court in Spain, or in America would believe it. You—
yourself if in a jury box would believe it. Listen to it—and then say
whether you would be declared innocent.

Inez,—You cannot frighten me. The courts of Spain will defend
the innocent.

Count,—Does this sound like innocence? A Baron of enormous
wealth in the prime of life goes to America, sees a singer in a little chapel, a girl not twenty years old, and of wondrous voice and beauty. This
girl's whole life has been spent among those who live in garrets, frequent
low concert halls and variety theatres of the commonest order, and who at
the time the Baron saw her was living in a garret, singing in that choir,
but whose every dollar was saved to purchase dress, not to wear then,
but to fill a trunk, with what purpose none knew but herself. But this
she did day after day—for the detectives tracked her doing it. One day
magnificently dressed she joined the baron up the Hudson, stays at the
same hotel with him, calls him Mr. Engaltare, the manager, tells every
one—she is going to Europe with him, that he has engaged her as a prima
donna. She goes to England with him, without even a female servant.
The baron is taken suddenly sick while on the voyage, has to stop when
the ship arrives,—she still with him.

The Baron in that hotel gives her deeds to a vast property. A violent scene ensues when they are alone, the people in the hotel hear her loud and angry voice, but no voice of his is heard by them.—In a short time, to the astonishment of all, the baron calls the people back, and they are married, and the only one to give her away was her servant. She asking him to do it. The ceremony is scarcely over before the baron tells a lawyer to put her name in his will, signs it, and falls dead. She pretending to faint. She comes to Spain under the further pretence of seeing the baron buried.—One night a man is seen to go into her room at the hotel. The only man that ever went there before. This man turns out to be her own father who had only been out of prison two weeks, after serving fourteen years for murder. Who she said died when she was five years old. But instead of being dead he was a convict, and she comes to Spain two weeks after his release. Her father was not dead then, though he is now—

Inez,—Dead now ;—Is he dead?

Count,—He is. Yes, he is dead, and there is the purse you gave him. His companions (convicts like himself) killed him last night for the gold that was inside it—

How now? what will a Court say to that? How about your innocence now?

Inez,—Oh! God! Oh! God, what is to become of me?—Monster, you murdered him, finish your work! Kill me! But before you do, know one thing, you will never touch the wealth you steeped your soul in blood to get!

Count,—No necessity of your dying? Marry me, and you are safe. Refuse me, and you die --

Inez,—Marry you? be bound to you? Have to call you husband? You— —I'd give up all the wealth of earth--and die ten thousand deaths before such a wretch as you should call me wife.—Out of my sight!—(*Draws a stiletto*)--Or I'll send you down so deep in hell, that a lead line could not reach you in its hissing flames. Go, viper, perjurer, murderer! Go!

Count,—No, but you shall go!

Takes out his whistle, blows a loud note.

Enter OFFICER *with* SOLDIERS.

Officer,—(*To* INEZ) You are my prisoner.

Inez,—For what ?

Officer,—For conspiracy and poisoning—by which means you procured the wealth and title of the Baron Engaltare, a Spanish nobleman, whose government now arrests you.

Inez,—I am an American—

Officer,—That gives you no right to poison a Spanish nobleman, and by your hellish deeds acquire his wealth and name.

Inez,—Who dare say this?

Count,—I do, his next of kin, Alphonso, Count Diego.

Inez,—You lie. You double dyed damned villain !

Tries to reach with her stiletto raised to strike him. She is seized, disarmed and handcuffed. As soon as she is ironed she becomes like a statue.

Count,—To prison with the murderess !

Enter DENNIS.

Dennis,—My lady—(*Throws off his coat and rushes towards her. The* SOLDIERS *keep him back.*)

Inez,—Stop Dennis. (*To the* OFFICER)—May I speak to my servant?

Officer,—Go to her. (DENNIS *approaches her.*)

Inez, -(*Aside to* DENNIS) Go for the baron's lawyer, in London. Tell him to come to me—

Count,—Take her away—(*They march off with her.* INEZ *stops, turns, looks at the* COUNT.)

Inez,—Coward, perjurer, murderer? How I loathe you!

End.

SCENE II.

Act III. Scene III.

Chancery Lane in London.—Sign on door of a house,—Law Office.—
Cummings, *solicitor.*

Enter Dennis.—*Looking at the house.*

Dennis,—Here's the house. Law office Cummings & Son. He's the man.—It won't take him long to get her out.—

Knocks hard and fast—Servant *opens the door.*

Servant,—Why don't you break the door, at once, and be done with it? Who do you want?

Dennis,—The big lawyer.

Servant,—You'll find him in the grave yard.

Dennis,—Dead? (*Staggers against the door post.*)

Servant,—An what would he be doing in the grave yard if he weren't dead? (*Slams the door and exits.*)

Dennis,—Oh! what will become of me poor dear lady now? The heart is gone out of me entirely. (*Sinks down on the ground, his back against the house as if almost fainting.*) What will I do at all,—at all? Dennis, Sir—(*talking to himself.*) Take a restorer.—(*Takes out a bottle, drinks, puts it back.*) That's a great medicine for an Irishman—me blessing on the doctor that first prescribed it. I feel better already. Arrah! what am I to do at all, at all? Dennis, Sir. Ask who attends to his business. (*Goes to door, knocks fast and loud.*)

Servant *opens door.*

Servant,—And is it you again? I thought it was the Prince of Wales. —What do you want now?

Dennis,—Who tinds to his business since he's dead?

Servant,—He has no business since he's dead.

Dennis,—You almost killed me with the scare you gave me.

Servant,—What if I had? There's too many Irishmen in the lane now?

Dennis,—Arrah! an I'm in too much trouble to quarrel with you.

Servant,—What ails you?

Dennis,—A set of murdering devils have got my mistress in jail in Spain. She sent me here for Lawyer Cummings to get her out. Now he's dead, what I'm to do at all, at all? I don't know.

Servant,—Is she a Spaniard?

Dennis,—She a Spaniard? She's an American lady from New York.

Servant,—From New York?

Dennis,—Yes.

Servant,—The American Minister is the man to get her out. Go to him. (*Shuts the door in his face.*)

Dennis,—(*In the lane*) The American Minister? He must mane Father Cregan. These Englishmen know no better than to call a priest a minister. (That's owing to the education they get, the poor ignorant creatures!) Faith, then, Father Cregan sure is the very man to go to--Who knows her better? Divil a one! And don't Father Cregan know the Cardinal? One line from him telling them she was innocent would turn her out? I'll be bound it would. Dennis, Sir! Take the train to night.--"The flying Irishman" (as they call that train for Cork) will put you on the steamer for New York--be two o'clock- and be to-morrow night you'll be out at sea. Roche's Point away behind, and New York in front. This is Thursday. You'll see Father Cregan on Sunday week. Dennis, Sir! That's your road! Go to the American Minister!

Scene ends

ACT. III.

SCENE IV. *Father Cregan's Library in New York.*

Enter Dennis.

Dennis,--Here I am at last, and it's wake I am with the sea sickness. It's time for Mass to be out. This Sunday makes seventeen days since I left me lady in the hands of them villains, and here I am,--thanks be to God!

Enter Father Cregan.

Father,--Why, Dennis, where did you come from, and where is your lady?

Dennis,--From Spain, where she is in a dungeon, the innocent darling, charged with getting the baron's property by poisoning him.

Father,--Monstrous lie!

Dennis,--True for you, and I come to get you to go back with me, and put the lie down their throats.

Father,--Why did not you go to the baron's lawyer instead of coming here?

Dennis,--So I did; she sent me to him; but he is dead, and his man sent me to you, and I never stopped night or day to get to you, except when I was stopped on the wharf this morning by a custom house officer [bad luck to him!]

Father,--That was right; they always search the baggage of the passengers.

Dennis,--But there's reason in all things,--divil a baggage, had I but a few things tied up in a handkerchief. As soon as the ship touched the wharf off I jumped, and was running up to you. Stop! says a chap with brass buttons. What for? says I; I'm in a hurry to see Father Cre-

gan, says I. I must search your baggage, says he. Take it all, says I,
but don't keep me waiting, says I. Have you anything valuable? says
he. I have, says I. What is it? says he. The right to vote the democ-
ratic ticket, to turn the likes of you out of office, says I. Get out, you
Mick, says he, and wait now until all the baggage is passed before I pass
yours, says he. Will I? says I throwing it at his head. There take it,
says I, distribute it among yez all, says I. The shirt is good, but it
wants washing, says I. The collars will do to light the stove, says I.
They're from the Boston paper mills, says I. You can take or leave
the handkerchief after you're done wiping your eyes, says I. And off I
goes up the wharf with all the boys around me crying, Want a hack, sir?
I saw Jim Daly outside with his horses. Jim, says I, jumping upon the
box beside him, drive as fast as ye can to Father Cregan's, says I. And
sure enough he did, and here I am for you to go back with me, and get
her out. Jim told me on the way up that a steamer goes out to-morrow
at 3 o'clock, so be the time the lamps are lit you and I will be passing the
Hook, and I'll wait on you myself all the way over and back. Now that's
settled. I'll pack your valise and go on your errands, so you'll have nothing to detain you.

Father,--But what can I do?

Dennis,--Get her out! Of course, you're the man to do it.

Father,--Me?

Dennis,--Yes, you! Who else? Listen till I tell you the whole of it.
The details I'll tell you on the way over. If you don't go they'll kill her
entirely--entirely. Thinking that that will give them the money,--but
it won't; it's all in bonds in New York, and none can get a cent of it unless she's here to draw it herself,--they have played all sorts of mischief
on her.

Father,--If she dies without a will, and leaves no heirs at law it
would all go to the State.

Dennis,--That's as much as to say the politicians will get it all. Now
I lave it to you, isn't it yer duty to stop that? Go and bring her back
home, and when she gets here she'll draw the money out and send enough
over there to build a church in thanks to God for her deliverance. She'll
build an orphan asylum here, and lave the Sisters money enough to take
care of them. And for your trouble, and to pay your parish for the loan
of you (if you get her out soon), a new organ for the choir she used to

sing in--you want one badly, the pipes are worn out in the ould one--
There now, ain't it your duty to go? Say the word! Expenses for
yourself there and back, and me to wait on you,--what more could
any parish want for the loan of a priest?

Father,--But I don't see what good I could do by going? If I could
save her I'd walk there to do it, if I could.

Dennis, -The steamer is easier, especially as there's four thousand
miles of sea to cross over. Father, dear, will you go?

Father,—But, Dennis, what can I do?

Dennis,—Get a line from the Cardinal. Do you think they'd gain-
say the likes of him?

Father,--But what could the Cardinal write?

Dennis, [*hands him a paper*]-- Read that. I wrote it on my voyage
over. I was the whole way composing it. Just let the Cardinal put his
fist to that, give it to you, and you put on your best coat, and give it to
them, and she'll be out while you'd be mixing a punch Just read it, your
Riverence, if you doubt my word.

Dennis,--My glasses are in the next room. As you wrote it you
had better read it.

Dennis [*reads,*]

To the Spaniards that has her:--

Turn her out; she's an innocent creature, and a good Catholic.
Turn her out, and when she gets back to New York, where every
cent of her money is (and no one can draw it but herself) she'll send
money enough back to build a good, dacent sized church at whatever place it is wanted, and yourselves to have the contract for building it, including the stone, bricks, and morter, the carpenter's work,
sidewalks and fences. But if you dare to kill her, you thieves of the
world, I'll fix the last one of you. Turn her out.

The Cardinal.

P. S. Turn her out, or I'll let the Yankees take Cuba, and free
all the nagurs. It's all I can do till return mail to keep them from
doing it now. They're so mad at your touching her.

No. 2. *P. S.* Turn her out immediately. I send Father Cregan for
her [and a dacent man he is]. Now if you don't give her to him
when he hands you this as soon as I hear that she ain't out I'll go

over myself, and take General Grant with me, as he is disengaged at present, and we'll batter the town down 'round your ears. For the way you have treated an innocent American female.

Mind that!

The Cardinal.

Father,—Dennis, keep that letter for the present. You and I will go to Washington to-night. I'll see Mr. Evarts; I think he'll do better than the Cardinal. We can come back to-morrow night, and go on Tuesday's steamer.

Dennis,—And you'll go with me then to save her ?

Father,—I will go, and do all I can.

Dennis,—God bless your Riverance !

Father,—God save her, and bless us all !

Dennis,—Amen !

Father,—You must be hungry, and tired, my poor fellow! Come with me.

[As they go out.]

Scene ends.

Act III.

Scene V.   *A Prison.—Inez a prisoner, condemned to die.—Re-clining on a straw bed on the dungeon floor.*

Inez.— Six weeks ago I was free, planning how to divest myself of riches and of title, and now,—here—in this dungeon condemned to die, to die to-morrow,—can God be just to let me die and that villain live who swore my life away? Is there no hope for me? Must I die—die—no, not die but be murdered? And is my young life to end thus? My God, my God! Is there no help?

Dungeon door opens. Enter Dennis, dressed as the Jailor, with a lantern in his hand and the prison keys. He puts down the lantern, and disguises his voice.

Dennis,—Shall I bring you some more bread and water?

Inez,—I do not want it.   I require food for the soul, not for the body.

Dennis, [*in his natural voice,*]—Poor creature, God help her!

Inez (*thinks she recognizes Dennis' voice*)—That voice,— —speak again—

Dennis [*disguises his voice again*].—What is it? What did you say?

Inez,—That is not the voice I heard. Has my brain joined my foes? Is it to deceive me who is deceived by all.--forsaken by all, even by Dennis?

Dennis,--(*Speaking in his natural voice*). Oh, blessed Virgin, shield her!

Inez,--There is that voice again. Oh! speak once more like that! Speak, oh! speak again!

Dennis [*cannot control himself longer*],

Dear Jasus, save her!

Inez,--Dennis!

Dennis,--Whist! or they'll hear us!

Inez,--How did you get here?

Dennis,--I'm the jailor!

Inez.--You?

Dennis,--Yes, me. Father Cregan got me the place this morning. The priest gave me a note to the Governor to hire me in the place of the ould jailor who was promoted yesterday to a bigger situation Father Cregan did that much for him. So you see he had one promoted, and the other appointed. The appointed one is me,--do you mind that now? Ar ah! Let Father Cregan alone; he's no fool! Devil a fool!

Inez,--Father Cregan?

Dennis,--Yes, Father Cregan. God bless the good ould priest! He's here!

Inez,--Here? How came he here?

Dennis,--(*aside*), I must brake it easy to her, or it will be the death of her. The Pope sent for him to consult with him about the crops He's on his way back now, and stopping over here to rest awhile.

Inez,--Send for him to come to me. Tell him I'm to die to-morrow.

Dennis,--Don't be so sure of that; you don't want the last rites yet, and you're not likely to, until you're oulder than my ould mother was when she died, and she was eighty-two. God rest her soul!

Inez,--What mean you? Is there any hope?

Dennis,--Of course, there's hope! Plenty of it!

Inez,—Am I not to die to-morrow?

Dennis,-Divil a die ! You'll be out of here to-night, and on the sea, before the morning as free as a sea gull !

Inez, --Free ?

Dennis,—Free, I tell you. What else brought Father Cregan here but to free you?

Inez,—To free me? And can he?

Dennis,—Arrah ! Ain't he a priest? Can't he do anything ? Who took yez from the Varieties to the chapel choir? Wasn't it he ? Who took yez from the chapel choir to fortune and to iligance? Wasn't it he? And wasn't it he who tould the baron who yez was? Wasn't it he who tould him to marry you? Wasn't it he? And what did he get for it?— Divil a more than the finishing of his new chapel. And isn't it his business now to take yez back safe and sound to America where he sent yez from ? And what is he to get for it ? Only the blessing of God, and that he can give himself; yet a trifle you ought to give to build a chapel here, in praise of your deliverance and the founding of an orphan asylum in New York with money enough for the sisters to take care of it, and expenses for himself here and back, and me to wait on him and if he does the matter nate and dacent and in a hurry a trifle more for a new organ. That's all, and that's the way he came here, and that's the way you're going out of here, and when you're back home I want the money to pay the bills.

Inez,— How do you know all this?

Dennis,—Know it? Ain't I the man who made the bargain?

Inez,—You?

Dennis,—Yes, me. I made it in New York, and brought the good ould priest with me. And he'll get you out of here, and when you're out I want the money to pay the bills.

Inez,--Take all I have but save me.

Dennis,—Not a cent more than the bargain shall any of them get.

Inez,—Oh ! you good man ! And I in my misery thought that you had deserted me.

Dennis,—Desart you? When did you ever know a rale Irishman desart a friend or a female?

Inez,—Forgive me! Tell me all.

Dennis,—Well, my lady!

Inez,—Call me Inez. Titles are mockeries here.

Dennis,—I went to London as you bid me. The baron's lawyer was dead, his son told me what to do—to see the American Minister, (of course he meant Father Cregan), so I went to America for the Father and here we are, he and I. The Father, as I told you, had me appointed to this place. This morning the Father says to me, Dennis, says he. Sir, says I. The American Minister has fixed it all, says he, giving me a wink, but for fear he should fail, says he. Who? says I. The American Minister, says he (winking again). I'll tell you what to do. I will, says I. Then, says he, a man will come to the prison, and say, "Jailor, the Father sent you this; take what he gives you, and do as you're told." I will, says I. Do, says he, and your mistress will be on her way to New York to-night.

Inez,—To New York to-night?

Dennis,—That's what he said. Are you sure? says I. Sartin, says he. Good for you, says I. The money is ready when she gets to New York, and I'll be listening to the new organ, says I. You will and to her singing, too, I hope, says he. Give us your blessing, Father, says I. Wait till I get the organ, says he laughing. But seeing me hurt at his doubting me word, I'll throw you in one now, says he, for nothing. So he gave me his blessing, and here I am, and you'll be out of this to-night.

Door opens, enter Prison Messenger with a basket, loaves of bread on top.

Jailor, the Father sent you this.

Puts down the basket and exits. Dennis rushes to the basket, throws out the loaves of bread, takes out from the bottom a cloak and hood, opens the cloak; a letter falls on the floor. Dennis picks it up and reads.

Put the cloak and hood on her. Let her take the basket on her arm, and walk out boldly with you. They will think that she is the jailor's wife. Go straight to the steamer. We will be at sea, and on the way to New York in an hour.

Inez,--Give me the things.

Dennis helps her on with the cloak, puts the hood over her head. She takes the basket on her arm.

Dennis,--Now follow me. Walk like if you owned the prison and was going to discharge the Governor. Come !

They walk towards the door, and are close to it, when it is suddenly thrown open, and the Count Diego appears, two guards with him.

Count,--Stop!

Inez (drops the basket, the cloak and hood fall off.)--Lost ! Lost ! Lost !

Count,--Bind that traitor!

The Guards seize Dennis.

Dennis,--Oh ! you spawn of Oliver Cromwell ! If I ever do get you in New York--

Count,--Take him away !

They are carrying Dennis out chained, and are close to the door, when the door is suddenly thrown open, and soldiers march in, led by the American Minister and the Officer of the Day.

Officer of the Day [to the Guard and Dennis],--Loose that man !

Officer [to the Count Diego].--I am ordered to arrest you for the murder of Juan De Plata and for perjury and conspiracy.

[Two of the soldiers seize the Count.]

Officer, [To Inez,]--Baroness, I am ordered to read you this, and deliver it to you.

(Reads),--Inez, the Baroness Engaltaie, is hereby fully pardoned, we being satisfied of her innocence. The Officer of the Day will deliver this in person to the Baroness, and see to it that she is delivered to the American Minister with all honors.

The King.

(As soon as the name of "the King" is spoken the soldiers present arms.)

Officer (hands Inez the King's pardon),

Baroness, you are now free and your innocence declared.   As ordered I deliver you with all   honor   to the American Minister here present.

American Minister,—My dear lady, I am thankful   and   rejoice to see you free.

Inez (falling on her knees,)—Free!   God is just!

American Minister,--Protected by Him and this.

(Displaying the American flag)

CURTAIN.

www.ingramcontent.com/pod-product-compliance
Lightning Source LLC
Chambersburg PA
CBHW022154020726
47496CB00008B/2712